Millie's Diary

Olean Hardaway Scott

GLOBAL
PUBLISHING
SOLUTIONS

MILLIE'S DIARY by Olean Hardaway Scott
Published by Global Publishing Solutions, LLC
923 Fieldside Drive
Matteson, Illinois 60443
www.globalpublishingsolutions.com

Cover design by Staci Marajh

Library of Congress Control Number: 2021912720
International Standard Book Number:
978-1-7372244-2-6
E-book International Standard Book Number:
978-1-7372244-3-3

Printed in the United States of America

Thanks to Mary James, a true friend and teacher, and Gwendalyn Mitchell, for her support encouragement. Special thanks to my parents, Rev. Booker T. and Alberta Hardaway.

*Let us share our time and wisdom to make
a brighter future for all children.*

Table of Contents

Introduction

The main character, Millie, a young girl, writes in her diary her dreams of a better way to live in a world full of an excess of everything. Millie is confident and driven to seek a better life in the story, apart from how she's living. She somehow knows that she should live her life fully and not merely exist. As a bright, curious child, she's determined to find answers. Nothing will stop her from thinking positively about her future, despite her negative experiences. Millie finds pleasure in discussing topics that often are far from the average child's mind. However, she remains in touch with her age level and communicates on their level.

Millie is a child expressing the true feelings and hopes of the young black girl in America. This little girl, who has many gifts, is a child with dreams, and as she grows, she learns more about life and the answers to fulfilling those dreams. However, dreams have very little value in this child's mind because Millie is like most children growing up in poverty—they seldom dream. She imagines a better world that lives within her perfect world of thoughts. While planning to be the one who breaks through the chains of poverty and reaches out to help others left behind, Millie is concerned that most children have forgotten how to dream and that they need a vision of living in a better world.

Preface

In the book *Millie's Diary*, you will find hopes and dreams turn into something colorful and full of life-giving energy, encouraging children to excel to the highest heights and know that there are no limits when you believe in yourself. Daily journal writings help to keep Millie focused. Millie is a child of today. She looks inside matters of the heart. Millie defines and presents truth as it is, with a brilliant photographic image of how children should live. Her character speaks on many levels as she grows up and experiences different facts of life. She waits to see change come to a world in desperate need of love and unity.

Chapter One

WAITING FOR SOMETHING BETTER

In a small town in Gary, Indiana, a young girl named Millie must live a different life than many children her age. It's an experience one never forgets. Millie had only three crackers to eat. Again today, she has to feel the pains of hunger. It's all the food they have left, and her mother keeps running downstairs to look for the check. It's a day late, something they have gotten used to after the major holidays. The people at the child support agency say it's on the way and that she should not worry.

It's kind of tough when you're a kid and can't have three meals a day. Worst of all is when we don't get much of anything. We're happy to get three crackers.

This lack seems like a dream, the kind I keep trying to get out of and can't. It doesn't seem to be the natural way for people to live. I feel bad not having nice clothes and shoes like other children. I say that it isn't fair for some children to be so hungry and all the wealthy and rich children I see on television to have all the food in the world.

Sometimes the children talk about the food they have for dinner, and I just look at the ground and wonder what in the world is under it, maybe some sister and brother. I know it is a lot of something inside the earth because it's mighty big.

My mind keeps telling me to act like we got food because they will never know if they don't go home with me. I say to myself, Millie, one day, one good old day if I live, I'm going to have everything I ever wanted.

I keep looking up at the clear blue sky and saying, God, I know there's some food enough to feed my sister, brother, Mama, and me. I know it's sufficient up there if it isn't in the ground. I feel better whenever I look up at the sky. I don't know why, but I do. Mama says not to think too hard about what's on the other side of the fence. It could be worse than the side we're on. Still, I believe and pray every night and say, dear Lord, show me a better house. Mama doesn't think there's anything left down here for us, especially food. We never get enough to eat in our home. Maybe if we got another one, it would be better.

Sometimes at Christmas, Mama says she will give us three toys apiece, but when Christmas comes around, we are lucky to get one thing to play with and some candy and fruits. I tell myself that's okay because we don't have fruits that often, and sometimes we get a turkey if it's enough money left after paying the bills.

My birthday came the other day, and my Grandma baked me a cake. She said someday she thinks she can take us to Disney World. I'm twelve years old and still waiting to see

Mickey and Minnie Mouse. They make me happy whenever I see them on television. I look outside when the rain comes down. I like how it makes the street look shiny and silvery all over. It's fun to make believe while looking out the window. I have one friend, and she is gone to live with her cousins for the summer. Her name is Rosa. I can't wait for her to come back. We catch lightning bugs and find four-leaf clovers. We have a contest to see who finds the most. That's the lucky person we always say. Sometimes Rosa has the most, and sometimes I have the most.

When I find things, it makes me happy. When I find money, I feel thrilled. I tell Rosa that we have to look for more four-leaf clovers. Maybe the good fairy will come along and grant me a wish. I will ask to be the wealthiest person on earth, and all the children will get toys and food whenever they ask. There would never be poor, hungry children again. It makes me happy to see pretty things, so I create my own by drawing and coloring them the way I choose. Paper dolls are one of the best things I have in my collection to keep me company. I miss my friend Rosa a lot. We used to study and do our homework together. I like to hear myself read because it makes me feel brilliant.

Sometimes my Grandpa asks me to read the newspaper and letters for my Grandma and him. It's fun. My Grandma

Lois likes to hear me read letters from her sisters and friends. They say their sight is failing and that they need to keep me around. Sometimes Mama tells them no because she needs me to help my brother and sister learn how to read.

I'm the baby of three, and the first is a pre-teen. I know she can read, but she acts like she can't read to keep them from asking her to come over to their house and read to them, especially with Mrs. Calhoun, because she needs somebody to read for her all the time. It doesn't seem to make sense because her letters are always from the same people—her children and sister. They say the same thing all the time. Monee thinks she can't take it anymore, so I have to be the one to read. She started paying me because she says nobody else can read like me. Anyway, she is too old to read to herself, and I guess she is glad to hear the same thing. Yet, still Monee can't take it anymore.

Sometimes I dress and run outside early to play jump rope. I go back inside when the sun gets too hot, and I get some ice and lay down. Sometimes Mama has a cold watermelon in the refrigerator. She slices it for us. We all get big slices. I love it when she has money to buy things. Once we needed money, Mama said we should look inside the couch, and under it, we found three dollars and some change.

We had enough money to buy bread and lots of candy. She says God always makes a way to feed children.

I still wish for all the things we need. It just doesn't seem like the right way for children to get acquainted with a big world and everything in it. Mama talks about her father sometimes, not a lot, but the things she says are good. She says he worked very hard as a construction worker, building houses and tall buildings.

He died because he didn't know he was sick. I didn't understand anything then because I was too young. I can remember very little—the picnics and carnivals we went to and having good food all the time. Mama says Dad was a real man. He always told the people to keep praying and working because they would be happy to see the good things happen from working hard.

The people in the neighborhood liked him. Mama said he was always helping others fix things in their houses. I know we cry more now since we don't have food and money. Mama is sad most of the time. When the check was late again, she got so mad that she screamed to the top of her voice, sat on the floor looking up to God, and said her children were hungry and needed food to eat. Hollering and screaming made her feel better. Then she got up from the floor and started looking out the window, hoping to see the mailman come with the check. She would walk through the house and pray, and we didn't know what to do. We were just some hungry little children waiting for somebody to do something that made a difference in our lives.

Mama hated to ask Grandma for money, but she had no other choice sometimes if the check was late again. I felt sorry for my Mama sitting on the floor crying because her children were hungry. That was sad. My brother Tony was funny. He would be the one to suggest to Mama what we could eat since we somehow kept bags of popcorn and peanut butter. He said we could have popcorn for breakfast and lunch and then peanut butter for dinner. That would get Mama to laugh. Then we all started laughing, and things were back to normal for a while.

The popcorn was always a treat, no matter when we ate it. We sang, read a good story, and danced our dance. I would read my poems. It seems like we gave Mama some energy, and sometimes she played with us. That was fun. I always wondered what caused the good times. Sometimes our house was full of other people's children. Mama would babysit to make extra money, make clothes on her sewing machine, and do cleaning jobs whenever she could. She tried with everything she had to make ends meet and make life better for us after that awful day when Dad died.

She said she decided to go and ask for work no matter what it was, as long as it was enough to feed us and keep a roof over our head. She was no longer afraid to let the people know she was in need. When Dad was alive, she was spoiled and never had to ask anybody for anything. That's how it is when the sky turns gray, but now it's blue. There will be no more hand-outs, she said. She pulled us into her arms and gave us a special hug. We felt safe and like things would be all right then.

School is fun. I learn a lot from my teachers. Life is getting better, and Mama is working full-time at a bakery. We get lots of bread, cakes, pies, and cookies. I share with my friends at school sometimes. When our grades are excellent, Mama rewards us with more cookies than we usually get. Monee never stays home. She leaves Tony and me to do all the babysitting. She had her mind on the boys, and they were also thinking about her.

Monee is cute with long hair and a keen face. She thinks she's the beauty queen of all times. I would tell her she's not, and we would get into a big argument. Then I would say she will never be as cute as me, and we would get into a big argument until she walked out, saying I was too smart for my good. I loved it when she said I was smart because I know I'm smart. My little sister Tess and brother Tony wanted to go outside to play a lot, but I had to hold them down on the floor or the couch and tell them Mama would whip them. They would scream, kick, and holler all the while till they fell asleep. When Mama came home, she would find us lying right there on the floor or on the oversized couch.

Mama said we got our height from Dad. She was of average height, and I was tall like Monee. Tony and Tess were average like Mama. I could pass for an older girl whenever I wanted to, and it was my way to a better world. Besides babysitting and taking children to school, I would say my first real job was at the neighborhood theater selling popcorn and candy. Then it was a fast-food restaurant.

By the time I was age sixteen, I had thought I was grown because of babysitting so much for my Mama and the neighbors, reading for everybody in the neighborhood, and teaching little children to read. Sometimes I acted as the teacher when I babysat and created a classroom with books and crayons.

I think something good will happen for me since I'm sixteen and have my job and own money. This is the first time I can go into a store and buy all the new fashions the girls wear in high school. I feel so happy now that I can wear new clothes. I'm still waiting to grow up completely. I guess the next few years to come will be lots of fun while I wait. I plan to go to college, get married, and then buy a big, pretty house.

Rain makes me relax and think about God and what he does all day long. I think about being good all the time. I know God loves me, and I like thinking about heaven. I enjoy reading my poem about friendship. Someday it will be a song. Sometimes, if I think badly, he would be busy helping somebody else, not me.

I love when it rains at night. I sleep well. Sometimes I think the rain is God's tears, which turn to white snow in the winter. Sometimes I wonder if he does it to make the world extra special and soft-looking. Now that I'm older, I look to the day I can go skiing and snowmobiling with my new friends.

One thing for sure, I can buy more of the things I want although it is just a tiny amount of money. I can still feel proud because I have the money to buy most of the things I dream of, like good food and clothes. I even dream of laughing in my sleep. I laugh and laugh. Lord knows I feel good then.

Things aren't been the same since Rosa moved to San Francisco. She was my best friend. Even though I didn't have much of anything at home, we laughed and laughed all the time. Rosa and I had lots of fun. The fun we had will stay in my mind till I see her again. She was my playmate, and I cried and cried when I found out she had moved away.

I'm still waiting for a good friend to talk with and go ice skating with in the winter. It's no fun to sit around the house and wish for your best friend to come back or play with your little sister and brother all the time. That can be very boring when you think about it.

Once Rosa wrote me a letter saying she was having all the fun in the world and missed all the children in the neighborhood and me. She said I should come there and live with her family. Rosa said life would be so good for me. Her letter sounded so good to me. I cried again and told Mama about her friendly letter, and Mama said, "Girl, don't get yourself upset reading a letter. You will have to go there and see for yourself before you believe what others say." I said okay because my Mama is smart. She knows everything. Anyway, I think she does.

After reading the letter, I wrote to Rosa and told her that I would come when school is out for the summer. Then I could see what she wrote to me about San Francisco. Even if nobody else could go with me, I knew I'd find my way there someday.

Chapter Two

THE BEST BUS RIDE

Today Millie decides to go to work with a brighter outlook. She could see some of the immense blessings on the way and thanked God.

"I now have work and a paycheck. How good can it get?" I thought.

It did get her a new wardrobe to start with, and then she was able to help her mother in small ways. With her mom, it was enough since it was only a part-time job. Millie became more determined to be a winner some sweet day. Many weeks passed, and the ride to work was always memorable. There were the same people and the same faces, but she could see through many big questions that filled her mind.

The other young students were always busy talking about their fun and the different boys they liked. Millie only thought about becoming successful someday. She knew there was a new friend and acted friendly with everyone.

Then one cool autumn day, she worked a different schedule and met up with two coworkers on the way to work. They had been working overtime for three days. They smiled and spoke to each other, and they sat together all the way to work. One of her coworkers was a promising college student with a great future as a scientist. His name was Monde.

We talked about many things, from the weather to different books we had read as we rode together. Melonie and Trisha both desired to become a teacher or doctor. I said my dream is to be the first female President of the United States. They all laughed as if I was kidding, but I let them know how I believed that the sky is the limit if you only believe in yourself.

They all agreed with me. I began to let my imagination run away for a minute, thinking of all the ways I would change the world and how all children would have the same educational chance as everyone else.

My friend and manager Monde talked about the science books he likes to read. He said he could just imagine how it would be with children reading good books everywhere.

Monde said he would write books that gave an authentic look on the inside of life. On their way to school and back home, Monde said that in his dream, there were smart children everywhere with great ideas and inventions to make a better world.

Monde said that science suddenly became a favorite subject. It seems like the world had changed suddenly, with children wanting everything scientific and whatever prepares them to be astronauts, doctors, teachers, meteorologists, or great writers. At Christmas, the stores ran out of new electronic games, which prepared the children to become future scientists.

Monde was in his first year of college and worked as a popular chain restaurant manager. On the way to work, we found ourselves laughing and enjoying each other like old friends. Life is getting better, and there seems to be something about my new friends. We all have a clear focus about our future. We all want a different life from what we had seen as little children.

Now I know why I had to wait for new friends to come along. We all are exceptional and from good families. Monde was always explaining the different homework he was assigned to do. That was very impressive, and I couldn't wait to get to college so I could brag about homework. He would say how some of the classes are very challenging, but he is prepared to go all the way until he becomes a biological scientist.

That's when Millie made up her mind to go straight to college after she graduates from high school next year. She is thinking about how cool he is and how he's brilliant. Now she can see her life in a greater sense than first imagined since Monde has become her tutor. Millie is thanking God for letting time work things out for her and for the special day he gave her to meet new friends on the bus.

Oh, Father Time, help me focus on each new day with a positive outlook on my future. Dear Lord, I ask you that my friends, those who have lived where I've lived and understand me, desire to make a difference in our community after reaching our success goals.

For now, I'm happy about the new friends I work with, like Monde, Melonie, and Trisha. They have lots of class and high goals. The best in the future is yet to come, and we have each other's phone numbers and pass along new information about work and school work. Monde doesn't talk that much, but Melonie, Tricia, and I enjoy each other very much. It's a beautiful start for the kind of friendships I want.

When Monde and I talk, it's mostly about school or the world's problems. He says there is not enough love demonstrated and that we need to possess agape love as the Bible tells us. Then maybe the world would be a happier place to live. I can see that we are becoming good friends. Mama sometimes tells me to get off the phone, do my homework, or cook some food for my little sister and brother. I say okay. Now that Monde, Melonie, and Trisha are friends, we must sometimes talk on the phone about homework and things.

But I soon forget what she said. It's not easy to stop talking when you are enjoying the conversations. After I finally get off the phone, Mama and I talk a lot about how the girls who want to make something special must be cautious and not become too interested in all the dating and stressful things of life.

I tell her how much I agree with her and how important my homework is for now. She laughs and gives me a great big hug. Someday I will talk to her about having my friends over for dinner and playing a few games. If children are close to people, parents should know all of them. I like all my new friends, and Mama will after meeting them. Monde is just the person to explain things about the universe since he loves science. Trisha and Melonie will keep everyone laughing about their hopes and wishes of teaching the world the real meaning of happiness and true beauty.

I have a treat for Mama. Someday, I will bring everyone over to our house, but for now, I think I will be slow and get to know them better before introducing them to her. I'm so glad that I don't have to wear a lot of makeup to look beautiful.

I learned to take care of myself, feel good, and exercise daily without spending lots of money on clothes and extra things to make myself happy. When you grow up poor, you wish a lot for almost everything beautiful. Since Rosa left, I'm delighted to meet new people that think almost like me. I think Monde is a great inspiration for the children, and he is the one to encourage them and set a good example for them. Knowing him will keep us all on the right track toward a good education.

I love to talk and talk and talk. Monde and the girls mostly listen to me. For some reason, I seem to like hearing myself, but the good thing about it is that I say many good things. Mama sometimes tells me to restrain myself from talking and to read a good book. Mama loves to read. That's great, but if I have somebody to talk about things, then I feel like someone cares about what I worry about and the things in life that make me wonder.

I'm still waiting to hear the boss say I can have a raise. I work hard and make sure the customers get their correct orders all on time. Since Monde is the assistant manager, I hope he gives a good word for me.

Everyone goes to him all the time to get a raise. Sometimes they get one, and sometimes they don't. I know my day will come. He already told me to be patient. Since he understands much of what I have experienced, he seems to care a lot. Both of us lost our dad while in grammar school. When Monde was eight years old, he says it was not easy losing his father. His mom also had a hard time raising him and his two sisters.

One of his sisters would stash food all the time and then eat it when everybody else went to sleep. He heard her crunching on potato chips one time, so he got out of his bed and crawled over to her bed and frightened her. She never hid anything from him again. From then on, she always shared whatever she had. That was a good story. We laughed and laughed.

He can tell funny jokes too. I want to hear whatever he has to say, funny or serious. I'm glad to have him as one of my good friends. Life is undoubtedly gotten a whole lot better since I started working.

As a little girl, I cried a lot. Everything seemed to be going wrong. There were more sad days, and I was fearful all the time. While in my bed, I thought about life and my classmates and friends. I believe the severe lack of food and clothes my sisters and brothers experienced was just a part of growing up.

Now I know that many children never go through different types of suffering. It's difficult for them to understand the feeling, but all children need to grow up with the sense of security and love of a family. I was almost falling asleep but heard the sound of sirens outside my windows. An ambulance stopped in front of our house. It scared me. I jumped from my bed and ran downstairs. Mama and some other people were outside looking around because they were trying to see what was wrong. It was the next-door neighbor's oldest daughter. She was about to have a baby. It frightened her, so she called the paramedics to come and take her to the hospital.

I went to my room and thanked God that it wasn't anything. I thought it was Grandpa. He always worked on things around the house and often got hurt. He once fell and fractured his hip. He retired and started doing minor things like repairing the sinks and electrical wirings because the doctors told him to stop doing dangerous work. He could fix almost anything you asked him. He's all we have now that we lost Dad. We're happy to tell people we have a grandfather. Mama has never asked him to do anything hard since he fell, but he loves doing small things like fixing the doorknobs.

Monde got a chance to meet Grandpa. Monde says he is a very great man because he tells about the things he can do. He likes talking about his young days.

Chapter Three

THE DREAM INSIDE YOUR HEART

Monde listens because he says there is nobody left in his house to talk to him about life except his mother, and she says she has just forgotten most things. Monde says it's because she had a lot of bad memories. She just gave up dating. She preferred to take care of them full-time. I told him he can always talk to my Mama because she will never forget her dating years. That seems to be all she talks about, especially when I have the time to sit and listen far into the wee hours of the night. Her stories are so funny. She made me laugh and laugh and laugh. We all enjoyed listening to her stories as we were growing up. Nobody can tell it like Mama.

For Thanksgiving, we invited Monde over to have dinner with us. It was wonderful to have him and my sister-friends over. It seems as though the food was better than ever. Maybe because I helped prepare some of the dishes. Oh, Father Time, help me focus on each new day with a positive outlook on my future and new friends. I feel like the future holds the best, and for now, I'll be patient since I'm still very young.

Today one of my new friends Melonie and I will go shopping for some of the small items we have on our list. Sometimes when we are talking, Mama says, "Girl, you need to get off the phone and rest your mouth for a while." She likes to remind me of the homework and house chores, but I keep talking and laughing a little longer. Sometimes if she is too tired to cook, she tells me to fix some food for my sister and brother. I told her okay and hung up the phone.

I'm happy to have Monde as my friend and tutor. He knows the answer to almost everything I ask about, like the time I wanted to see how a person could determine a person's intelligence. Well, he just handed me a Rubik's Cube and watched if I could work it. I did very well. He said that's how; just give them something to do. We laughed and laughed until I fell to the floor.

Monde gave me some excellent advice concerning my job. He said that the bosses come around to see if a person is putting in extra effort to show they care about their work. So I work as hard as possible, and I'm still waiting to hear from the boss. They give raises when you work hard and prove you are dedicated to the job. Sometimes I get tired of pushing those keys and ringing up orders. But that's the job they gave me, so I will just act like it's okay for now.

Soon I will get a better job after graduating from high school. I can just hear the sound of "Pomp and Circumstance" all in my head. My Grandma and Grandpa like to say that everything I want is just over at the rainbow, and you know what? I believe them. I can imagine all the great things about life. Mama says I have to be patient and believe. Mama says she likes my friends, but she knows I miss Rosa a lot. I got a letter from her saying she will return for the summer. I was excited to hear that.

Mama likes Monde a lot because he has good manners and is very intelligent. We laughed since we both talk about some people with bad manners, especially those who drop out of school and hand out on corners. It's great to hear her say something nice about my friends because she keeps a script in her head about everybody, even if they are nice. When she thinks something is wrong with them, I try to talk about all the good things about them. Mama got upset when they forget to take off their shoes in the house. She believes they are absent-minded because she has a note reminding them to take off their shoes. She says she works too hard to keep out the germs and keep the floor clean.

Mama always keeps a clean house, clean dishes, and clean dish towels for unexpected visitors. Also, she says I have to learn how to cook great exotic foods. It helps to learn about all cultures and the type of food they eat. I want a good husband someday. I laugh till my side aches. We have the best time together, especially when I get in the kitchen with her. That's where I learn all the good stuff about cooking.

Mama is the best cook. She always baked pies and cakes for people to make her extra money. Now she makes special foods for her friends on holidays.

I love all the different seasons, and the world looks so different during each one. Autumn and spring are my favorites. I like winter when it's not too cold. Rosa wrote a letter and told me winter is always great in California, never too cold. I know I will visit there very soon. Rosa and I plan to get our college degrees before we even think about marriage and children. Rosa said there are always different movie stars helping poor people get houses and better education. She says she even worked to sign up some young people who wanted to take extra credit jobs.

Monde says a little power and knowledge will always be the answer to staying in touch with your true self. He said God is always near the best creation he ever made. Monde knows a lot about life and says all people are special in different ways. The way we think and do things helps to make the world interesting. The natural environment, trees, mountains, oceans, and sun are God's handiworks. Monde goes to church, and he invited Mama and me to go with him. We both agree that we will visit one day. I told him I need to buy some new clothes. But, he says it doesn't matter if the clothes are new or old, and it's all about growing to understand the more important things of life. Then people will eventually understand the truth.

I tell Monde I will have to buy something new because I like to look pretty whenever I go to church. He laughed when I told him that. Lately, my classmates talk mainly about the hard times they are having getting a good job to buy their prom clothes. I suggest they have someone make a specially designed dress. It will cost less and look terrific. I try to encourage them to keep looking and tell them that something will eventually come up. They say I hope you are right because the time is coming fast.

The good thing about life is that we can change things that are not right for us. My Mama always says it's a terrible wind that never changes. I know she's right because even a tornado can stop blowing.

Today I decided to walk down to the library and check out some good books about the planetary system and the incredible universe. I will be writing an essay about it. Everything I do must be excellent since I'm hoping to become valedictorian of my graduating class. I can just hear the sound of "Pomp and Circumstance" all in my head. When I told Monde why I need extra tutoring, he laughed because he thinks I don't need too much help since I get pretty good grades in algebra. Then he congratulates me for wanting to be better.

Monde says he plans to write some books about science. That's his favorite subject, and I love listening to him talk about the space program and all the different names of former spaceships. He knows the name of every astronaut that ever went into space. I tell him that maybe he will be our next great astronaut, and he laughs and says anything is possible. I want to write a few great books someday. Monde says he will write about the great people who have inspired others to succeed in their dream goals, like W. E. B. Du Bois, Frederick Douglass, John F. Kennedy, and Martin Luther King, Jr.

Sometimes I think about writing about children born to do extraordinary things, and for some reason, they get discouraged and lose interest. Mama tells me I can do anything I want to do. She gives me that serious look and pats me on the head. She says," Keep all that sense inside your head. Nothing is too hard, no nothing." She doesn't know about my horrible nightmares and the fear that lives down inside me. She doesn't know. I know that time doesn't

24

wait for us to grow up because before you know it, another year appears.

As I look in the mirror, I see a taller girl than last year. But, I know that my thoughts have not changed. All the times when Mama and my sisters and brother think I feel sick, they will never know my real secrets and fears. I pray to God for help. I used to hear Grandma pray, and I try to say what she said. I feel better then. I can keep one perfect thing—my dream to become someone special to help the world someday. I know dreaming is part of building the future with high expectations, and that feels good.

My friends and I talk about leaving Gary after graduating from high school. We plan to go to many places around the world. It's part of living and experiencing the more fantastic side of life. It's essential to learn about all the different cultures in our world. I have friends from almost every culture, and I have learned how to speak several languages. My school is very concerned about its children and how we excel in everything we aspire to achieve. I'll never forget Ms. Porter, one of my very favorite teachers. She knew my potential and was the first and only teacher to send me a birthday card in the mail.

I'll never forget her, and she never knew how my little heart began to heal as I read her card. It seemed to have a special healing effect that I cannot explain. I ran to Mama, jumping up and down and saying, "My teacher sent this pretty card to me!" The memories keep a dream in my heart.

Teachers are special to God. They seem to know what children need and bring out the best in their students. Ms. Porter always wanted me to be the class leader in reading, and most things I didn't think I could do because of the secret fears inside me. It's a reality that everyone has to come through a teacher in life, regardless of their profession. A teacher is someone responsible for our hopes and aspirations. They will be my reason for working hard and never giving up.

When I was little, I used to make play doll clothes. I learned how by watching Mama sew things. Making my paper dolls and cutting the clothes from the catalogs was a favorite of mine. I love beautiful clothes, and maybe someday I will be both a teacher and a fashion designer. Mama says whatever I desire will be okay with her. She says I will do a great job. I love my Mama. She is strong and beautiful, the kind that will be on my side no matter how I look or what I do. One more great thing about Mama is that she knows how to make me believe in myself, like when I said I want to be a famous fashion designer. She said, "Girl, you can be anything you want to be. Keep working at it."

Mama always says never worry about tomorrow. It will get better with each new day as long as you keep your mind and heart right. I learned how to listen to my Mama, and now I can face the world without expecting it to embrace me. Monde says he learned from his dad because his mom doesn't talk that much. She mostly read the Bible, other good books, and newspapers. She likes to sing songs all the time. My tutor says that college will be tough if I don't get the hang of it now. So I collect all the information I need from the internet and the library. It helps me a lot, and the best thing of all is that I will be familiar with the challenging part.

I think today's children will have the answers to a better world. I worry about all the great big puzzles of life and listen to my teachers because they are intelligent and perfect for children. Monde said a teacher shocked them by saying something so mean. He said the students looked at the teacher like he was a total stranger or something. I'm still waiting for things to get right. Then I think I'll be happy.

I think it's great to live a happy life and have most of the necessary things you need in life, and it's essential to eat right before going to school. A child with an empty stomach can't learn like a child who eats a healthy breakfast or lunch.

So many things are big puzzles in life, and I keep trying to figure them out. Mama tells me, "Girl, you need to relax and look out the window for a spell." I laugh and tell her, "I know everything that's going on outside those windows, so don't expect me to get involved in useless sightseeing." She laughs at me and shakes her head, saying, "Well, you are right on trying to figure out this great big world if you want to. I'll relax and take life easy since I've worked so hard to raise you all. After all, it's time for my children to become scientists and great leaders."

I tell her that will be very soon if I have my way. She says, "You have to compete with a world of intelligent people out there." I laugh and say, "Mama, you had a lot to do with giving me a large portion of my sense." Monde is brilliant too. Maybe he will be a great leader or something special, and perhaps it will be both of us.

Millie, a senior now, will be starting school. She's very excited about the classes she will take. After meeting new people, she'll be introducing them to members of the student council. She and Monde will need to meet in a week for tutoring.

When I was little, I used to like going outside to play. No matter what the weather, it was always better than staying in the house. Now that I have a part-time job and school, it's kind of hard because sometimes I just want to stay in bed and sleep like a bear.

Chapter Four

A LESSON FROM AUNT TESS

I remember asking my Aunt Tess why there is not enough food and houses worldwide. All she knew to say was that maybe some people were supposed to have less and that some don't have to work. I was a little girl then, and sometimes I think she was drinking what Grandpa calls moonshine because it didn't even make sense to me. I love asking questions, and Aunt Tess was the most intelligent person I knew next to my Mama.

One day she went to the riverboat and gambled all of her money away. Her poor kids were begging for food and money to buy something to eat, and all the people in the neighborhood knew about it. She started looking bad. She stopped combing her hair and putting on clean clothes. Mama said she was very depressed, and I thought it was a severe sickness. It could even happen to children, especially when they got a mama like Aunt Tess. I know that doctors can help people get over bad things like depression, and Aunt Tess is much better. She started wearing pretty clothes again and smiling a genuinely happy smile once again.

I can say now that I got the real Aunt Tess back who makes everybody laugh and visits the sick in the community.

She and Mama love doing this. They both started going to church. Aunt Tess stopped going to the riverboat casino because she knows how hard it is to not have food and the necessary things in life. After all, she's tired of losing all of her money and looking silly when the children ask for school money.

I'm no longer confused after asking Aunt Tess questions. She always makes sense now. Before she got help, Mama would tell me not to ask her any more questions about things because it could confuse me for the rest of my life. She can smile now because it's great to know recovery is possible as long as we hold onto life. She is doing better than ever. Aunt Tess sits on the porch drinking lemonade most of the time and waves hi to everybody she knows and to the folks she doesn't know. She's a funny aunt and nice to me. She goes to the health club all the time and asks Mama to go with her.

Mama says her exercise comes from cleaning up the house and walking to the store. They both are in their forties and look twenty. I tell them I want to be healthy like them. They say be careful who I marry, and they have a good long laugh and go out to dinner or shopping.

I like working because I can buy some of the things I see in the windows, but not everything, only enough to make me happy. It's fun to shop with my friends from school. They like to window shop and collect pretty shopping bags. They laugh and say it's cool to have the bags with popular names even if they are empty. We put our books inside to make them look full; collecting shopping bags was the way we could overcome our days of wishful thinking.

Wow! Those were the days. Now I can shop at those stores and buy myself some things, even if I only buy the smallest item in the store. If you want instant happiness, go window shopping and get yourself a great shopping bag.

The other good thing about life is feeling completely free to laugh, cry, and walk and run to wherever you want to go. It's a great big free world, and I'm learning that life's lessons come free. The world is the first university we have to get through. There are so many lessons to learn about life. I can hear the music from "Pomp and Circumstance." It's my beginning of life's true happiness.

You need faith in yourself and to believe. I know that deep down inside my heart. Sometimes I wonder how I know all the stuff I know. My friends listen to me when they have trouble keeping a boyfriend or a job. Most girls tell me they can't keep a job because they date the boys at work or think it's okay to talk a lot while working. I tell them they need to wait until break time to talk. Work is what helps everybody to have money. It's not about falling in love and talking all the time. I tell them this, and they say not one word. Sometimes they listen to me, and sometimes they don't

At sixteen, I feel smart. I can't say why, but sometimes I feel a special kind of job is waiting for me—something more than my chosen profession. I'm still trying to figure that out.

I've got to tell you about my cousin Shadee. The girl thinks the world owes her everything because of her looks. She says she has to get all the attention now because one day, she'll be too old to act the way she does now.

Shadee is three years older than me, but she always acts like a little girl. She thinks the boys prefer her to act immature, so she does all the crazy things they tell her to do. She runs the streets all hours of the night and sits on people's porches, having the owners run them away all the time. They throw rocks at cars and do lots of silly things. She's cute and all, but to tell you the truth, the girl is not all that at all. I tell her what I think. She says I'm jealous. I can't see what she means by that, so I go home and tell Mama everything she says. My Mama has a good laugh about the stuff I tell her about people, especially Shadee.

Mama says that girl is like her mama, Aunt Tess. She got everything honest, and nobody should expect her to be different from her mama. Girls need their mama to teach them about the natural way to grow up and be free in their minds and bodies and know how to communicate and enjoy each other as children. Boys need their dad to teach them how to be nice to the girls, and they should learn while young how to respect each other.

The primary things about growing up have to come from parents. I think parents should not overlook the critical times in a child's life. If they do, their kids will ask other kids, and the other kids will tell them anything. It doesn't have to be the truth, but they will believe it, and the other kids are glad someone is asking them something about the things only a parent should know.

One day Shadee and I went over to my boyfriend's house, and he wanted to rough house her a lot. I sat there looking at them act silly. I thought that they were the most ridiculous people I had ever seen. I said no when he tried to get me involved. He had Shadee rolling all over the floor, pulling her hair, and I couldn't see how this was supposed to be fun for a girl. A boy maybe, but not a girl. Gee whiz. I thought if that's having fun, then I'll never have fun with a guy, I mean never! I told her she looked like a silly ragdoll rolling all over the floor with him, like a little puppy or cat or something. She begged him to stop tickling her and making her stomach hurt. I said I got to go home, and Shadee hit him and said she was leaving with me. I told her she had some good sense then.

I'll never forget how silly they looked. On the way home, I told her, if you want to be pretty and make boys like you as someone special, you have to act special. Shadee was upset with me because she thought I talked too much. She thought I thought I was too cute to play games with her and her so-called boyfriend. She was real prissy-like. I told her that I'm much too mature for that now.

I never hung out with Shadee again after that unbelievable day. We speak, and all, but that's it. I'm pleased without Shadee going places with me. I stick to my classmates and Monde. They're all I need because we see life the same way. Monde likes to listen to me, and I like listening to him. Shadee is upset with me since I have new friends.

She still comes over to my house to talk sometimes, but all I have to say to her is that I'm happy with my classmates and new friends. Sometimes I think about the sense I have. I think I got a little more to take me through life, and God knew I would try to help other people like my cousin Shadee. I think they need a little help in seeing life as it is and not what society is doing. Kids sometimes do things like their aunts and other folks in their life, but I don't think that's a safe way to do something. Everybody is the keeper of their soul.

To go through life with a purpose is brilliant, but waking up and going through the motion without thinking isn't very smart. The problem with kids today is that they think they are smarter than their parents, but the truth is that kids learn a lot from their parents. I believe children should love their parents, be obedient, and think about how they got life and where all their good and bad sense originated. I know I can do many good things because my parents could. The gifts keep going through the family until somebody takes them and does something great with them. It doesn't stop at success; it goes on and on into generations of greatness, great wisdom, and strength to enlighten others. Mama says people learn from each other. That's the way it should be, the good and the bad, and it is mostly the bad that people remember about other people. They keep it in their head, motivating them to try and do better.

Little children sometimes go outside and learn how to say bad words. Then their mama asks them if they learned the words from the other children. If they say yes, then their parents try to stop them from playing with those children. Sometimes it works, and sometimes it doesn't. I wonder about growing up and becoming a mom because it's hard to keep your lovely little children from picking up bad habits from others, but I will be smart enough to do the job and marry someone who will be there forever to watch them grow.

Mama says homeschooling is a great way to keep your children from learning too much about the wrong things in life, being distracted a lot, or being influenced by the other kids.

Mama says the big people forget the children who have the worst problem growing up in the world. They write down the stuff that will help all the easier problems like temper tantrums. Often the children with extra energy are overlooked. I think they got a lot of sense and can do most things the other children do. Some children complain that no one listens to them, and then they do whatever makes them act out for attention. They need to feel happy inside like all the other children in school.

Sometimes the teachers stay home when they feel bad, and they say they get terrible headaches all the time. Some teachers work extra hard to keep the classroom in order. Children like having substitute teachers because they think they can get away with talking, playing, drawing, and going to the washroom. Most substitute teachers are friendly to children and let them do unique things in the class, like taking messages to the office or washing blackboards.

I'm not sure if schools should suspend children. In most cases, they are happy to be out of school, so there is no real punishment, and worst of all, they forget a lot of their classwork and fall far behind. When they come back to school, they can hardly remember anything. Teachers have to help them catch up with the back work. I think that's hard work for one teacher with a room full of children. Everything is rather scary. I don't know what the children of my generation think about success and excellent education. Most of them are too busy working and trying to make money for clothes and school.

I try not to think a lot about evil. I excel in my classes even though the world keeps changing. Therefore, I will be strong and live. War and hatred are everywhere. That troubles me. I wonder if there will be an answer to all the world's problems. I think that maybe my generation will find a solution. Mama says to not think about those things because God is in charge and that no one can change his plans. I keep saying to myself. I say, Millie, we got to learn how to love everyone, and the world will be a better place for the children who are on the way.

I learned early in my life to be grateful for the weather, whatever it may be, because the weather is real, and everything makes life worthwhile. New babies learn about eating and crying, and I still like eating and sometimes crying. It makes me feel better. I don't like crying when somebody says or does mean things to me. That's not a very good cry.

I like talking to my classmates about life and the beautiful things that make the world a wonderful place to live. When children watch bad t.v shows and movies, it gives them nightmares, and they are afraid to go to sleep. When I babysit or tutor children, unless it's educational, I refuse to let them watch t.v. They have parents who tell them how to watch out for drugs and alcohol. I like reminding them. I tell them to hang onto scary movies.

When I tell them this, they laugh and laugh, but they know I'm telling the truth. Sometimes they come back and tell me how it worked for them. We are seniors in high school. So far, the students are careful about making wrong decisions in their lives, especially things that take them away from homework or graduating, and marching down the aisle to the sound of "Pomp and Circumstance"! I'm so happy!

The boys and girls need to know they only have one life and one chance to take care of the beautiful person inside them; they need to love themselves first. I tell them that sooner or later, a very nice boy will appear like how it happened to me. Monde, Meloni, Trisha, and I went to a science fair the other day. We love attending science fairs. Monde said it gives him a chance to get better ideas. He knows he will be a great scientist someday. He studies a great deal in the library.

Chapter Five

THE BEST DAD

When times were good, I remember Dad talking to Mama about making life better for us. I remember the great stories he would tell and the songs he taught us. We sat around on the floor, eating our favorite snacks and desserts. That's where he and Mama talked about everything. He read the Bible verses, taught us great songs, and even recited Mother Goose rhymes. Dad had a gift of storytelling, and Mama would let him have his fun with us. She said she didn't know any songs to teach us. We looked at her and had a good laugh because we would always say that she knew everything. While cooking or working, she would sometimes sing her favorite songs, and we started singing with her. She wanted to give our Dad credit for it, and you know, I think that's all right since the fathers are extraordinary people in the family.

One winter evening, Dad came home and told us about a bad thing that had happened to some people not far from our house. The children had played with matches and set the house on fire. The firefighters tried to save it, but the house burned to the ground anyway. All the neighbors did what they could to help them out. They needed somewhere to stay, and different folks offered them a place till they could get on their feet again. My Dad took food and money over to help them. He was a very caring person. My Mama said life would not be as good if they had not met each other. My Dad cared about everybody. He was concerned because he had a good heart. He was loved and respected by all races of people. Mama says people love you quickly when you have a good heart and a friendly smile.

I remember my Dad shaking hands and laughing a lot with everybody in the neighborhood. I could have never imagined a better dad. Since it's been a world, people have been getting angry about things. Monde says the world is a good place. He says quiet people know a lot because they sit back and think about things. Most of the good things they think about will be written about someday. Sometimes I still think the world is a terrifying place, but I know those good people can help make it better if everybody works together.

I think a person should learn all they can from their teachers. Books help to put loads of good information into your head, and teachers want children to learn from them. I say to myself, Millie, you have to learn how to think things out for yourself. That's why there are school books. I'm so glad I know how to read, write, and think. A lot of information is in the history books. I read and write about many essential things at the library. That's how I know life is supposed to be remarkable. Nobody is going to make me stop learning.

When you become a high school student, you know a lot so that you can tell the younger children about it before they ever get to high school. Maybe they can have it better off than their parents. When thinking about when I was a little girl, I remember my Dad telling us to sit still because he was going to tell us a story about the Indians. He started telling the story so well that my big sister sat down on the floor and listened too. He told us many stories about all the good people he met and all the places he visited. I was always glad to hear him tell stories. That's why I love reading and spelling; I guess it comes naturally.

I love to learn about things because nobody can take them out of my head. If you put information into your head, it's there to stay unless you start doing harmful things and start forgetting everything you learned from using alcohol, abusing the body with drugs, or not eating right. I think the mind is like a computer. It can hold a lot of good or wrong information.

I believe it's a real shame when people forget the reason for the gift of life. My Dad said it's essential to work hard and be the best person you can be and that everyone has a gift. He said human beings come into the world to do great things and teach the children about the good they can do to become better people.

Today my friend named Sassie called. She is the funniest girl I know. To tell the truth, her whole family is funny. Everywhere you go, you will see someone from her family. I think it's about twenty of them in one house. They all love their mother. She raised all of them by herself because their daddy died and left everything to her.

She was strong and determined to raise them. They all are grown up now and still listen to her. She tells them they aren't too grown for her to knock them down if they even thought about saying something out of the way or disrespectful around her. Mrs. Drew was always telling how she and thousands of others with the civil rights leaders marched to get a better world for themselves and their children. That's why she tells them she demands respect at all times. I know how important it is to use all my thinking power because of how she talked about all the mean things that the people suffered.

Nothing will stop me from learning everything in the books and finding out what all the smart older people know. Sassie lives down on the other side of town. There's an old run-down hotel dividing the two sides of town.

Most folks living there don't work at all. Life is not very easy for them. Many of them stopped school early to work seasonal jobs in the factory. Most people did cleaning jobs and painting for someone.

When the work ran out, they had nothing to look forward to and began hanging out on the corner all day and night; they have given up on seeing things get better. I feel bad for how the poor suffer more and more each day. I was hoping for something to get right for them. For sure, children grow up and become great if they stay in school. I see it all the time on television and in books and magazines. That's why I love learning.

One of these days, my Mama will be proud of me. I said to myself, keep believing and never give up on your dream. I remember hearing Dad talk about the problems of poverty. He couldn't understand why many former soldiers are without decent housing and excellent jobs because they served their country with pride. Dad was proud that he served his country. He thought soldiers should have a better opportunity to live bravely and with dignity. Anyway, I'm happy that he liked being a construction worker. I miss having a dad. He was a real man. My Dad loved his family, and we loved him very much.

Chapter Six

MAMA'S STORY

Mama loves talking to me about growing up and all the beautiful things I can have. Sitting and listening to her is one of the best times of my life. She teaches me a lot about so many things. To hear Mama talk about her desires as a child makes me strive harder to achieve my goals. Mama wanted to have her piano, gave up the idea, and never got one. My dream is to buy her a piano.

I hear Mama talking to Aunt Tess on the phone, and they always talk about the bills and world problems. Sometimes they have a good laugh about something they heard on t.v. or something they have seen. I love to eavesdrop on their conversations because I learn a little more about grown-up life and their struggles. That's when I say to myself, never no, never will I go through such bad times. In life, you have to think about the future because that's the actual dream. Nobody can take that from you. You can speak it and then make it happen.

Someday all will see how you believed in yourself. Never giving up is the key. I feel so strong down inside me. I love my Mama. She's why I can dream a bit. She always asks, "Girl, where did you get all those big ideas?" I laugh and tell her she is my role model. She smiles, hugs me, and says, "Well, maybe you will be the first woman president someday." I get more confident about my future to hear that. I know I can be significant. I know it!

Mama has a few favorites of all my friends, and one of them is Sassie. She is one of the smartest girls on the other side of town. Sassie keeps a job and is always doing something special for her mother. She buys her gold jewelry and is nicely dressed for birthdays and holidays.

I think Sassie is going to be something special someday. She says she won't let the world hold her down. That's the way to think. I feel we're a little alike. We have to have a strong mind and a desire to be successful. Sassie makes me laugh all the time, and that's the kind of people I like being around. We know what we want and plan to go out into the world and get it. If a person doesn't get a good education and some special knowledge, they will end up standing around on the corner, looking silly—the kind of silly to make people ignore them.

One of the worst diseases for people is wasting their brainpower by doing nothing all day. Everybody should have something to do to keep the mind active, like reading good books or volunteering to do something for a great cause.

It's a great feeling to have a life and good friends who love and respect you. They help by sharing things. We learn a lot from each other. I laugh when my Mama and her friends get on the phone and call each other whenever they see somebody walking down the street wearing a new hat or new clothes. On the nights they don't have anything to do, they get a chair, start talking, and sit till they fall asleep. Sometimes they stay on the phone talking to each other until one of them falls out of the chair laughing so hard about something. They tickle me.

I tell my Mama she needs to join a club for the retired people. She says she will not sit around in no center knitting or doing art all day long. She says she would rather be out shopping and feeling free to be herself all day. I think it's a real shame to keep sitting around the house, looking out the window, and wishing all your life for small things like shoes and clothes that you are supposed to have naturally. Clothes and things are necessary needs, and it is a real shame not to have them. Mama says she came into the world to have some beautiful children to watch grow up and have a better life than herself. My Mama is so funny.

I think my Mama makes a lot of sense. She says children are supposed to have a good life and that parents should do everything to make it better for them. I plan to be successful because if I don't, my Mama will still be waiting to see her children be unique somehow. She says we got enough sense to be the President of the United States or the President of anything for that reason. I will keep working hard in school and get A's and all the awards for excellence in academics and leadership. I love being a leader. It allows me to share many things with the other students they don't know. Gee whiz! I keep hearing "Pomp and Circumstance" all in my head!

My Mama does have some work to do. It's not every day, but she's pretty busy sometimes. She works as a companion to older people. Sometimes they want to go shopping and to movies or excellent restaurants. She says she likes her job because it allows her to go places she has only read about or seen on t.v. Most of the little ladies are retired and have comfortable lives.

She says the food is always good. She never learned how to cook fancy food, and to go to better restaurants is like living the good life. If that's what makes her happy, I guess it's all right, but it's not the kind of thing I want to do for a living. I keep hearing "Pomp and Circumstance" in my head!

My Mama always says that Monde is a nice guy. She tells him he will be a great man someday if he keeps going to the library and researching. He has many ideas that will help make the world a better place to live. He knows he wants to be a scientist and help people get well, so his future looks excellent. Mama says good people come into our lives to tell us something we have to do and that we have to remember it because that's what will guide us into the future and the work that's cut out for us.

I think she missed her remarkable work, and she laughs when I tell her that. She told me a story about a friendly teacher in the fifth grade. Her teacher told her she would be a great actress someday if she had somebody to push her and encourage her.

Mama said she didn't tell her parents about a play because they were too tired to even look at the homework. They were working hard to make a living for the family. She knew they were too busy trying to make sure they had food to feed a house full of children. She stopped being in plays or anything special in school because my Mama has many stories to tell.

My Mama has a lot of stories to tell. She said most mothers are busy caring for their family and cooking so much that they forget about themselves. They never get a chance to live their dreams or buy pretty clothes they always wanted, especially if the daddies leave them holding an empty cup. Aunt Tess said one day she went out and bought some pants to feel like the boss in her house since she had to be the mother and the father. Mama was in the army as a young woman. She liked it because life then was more manageable with no real responsibilities, except to learn to be prompt, polite, and stable at all times. She said it made her super strong, but I wonder why she doesn't feel like it now.

There were different trades and professions to choose from, and she became a cosmetologist because she desired hair styling. She said she worked for a while in a shop, but mostly at home. I love the way she does my hair. I'm proud of her, but she will never work in that field again.

She now likes to talk about her crush on a boy that lived next door to her. She never told anyone before. He was a neighbor, and it was her secret. He liked her too. They dated a lot. He moved later on, and she never saw him again. Mama said boys listen to their mothers a lot and that most times, they want to play with other boys.

I get happy listening to all the stories. Most of all, it makes me determined to work for what I want, and it gives me the strength to do all it takes to stay strong. I know it's a terrible thing to be poor in the world. Some people don't see you as being necessary at all. Mama said some girls' families had money and were able to take care of their children.

Mama said her family was very good to them, and they had as much as the other children. Mama remembers when times were very hard, making her want a better life as she grew up. Her wishes and dreams were for her parents to someday live in a decent home. One day it happened. Now she's waiting to see her children's dreams come true as she knows they will. Everybody needs to have a plan.

Mama said most of her dreams came true, and she could tell others to keep hoping for the best. She said dreams have a way of becoming a future. We believe in them and work hard. I love listening to her talk. I hated to see the hard times come again after Dad died. She's unique, and life has a particular way of letting her know it.

Mama thought a lot about herself, and she was proud to get a job while in high school. I got my excellent work ethic from both parents. She says it was not easy because she had to help her family when the other girls played and had fun. Her stories help me stay focused on a better way of life. I think about the people who call me on the phone asking for dates. Since I know they are not serious, I laugh. I prefer not to talk a lot on the phone. I read a lot, but I do what I can to help folks like Shadee get into my little circle of friends and change. Girls have to be careful of the people they allow into their life especially if they aren't serious about school.

Mama says there's a lot she has to say to help other girls and me to stay in school, study, and keep our heads straight. I'm still waiting to hear the rest of her life stories. Sometimes I look at Mama and think she is extra special because she still looks young and pretty through all her complex trials. Life knows what she will end up doing in this world. I know so far that her life has not been like anybody I have read about or known.

It also bothers me when girls come to work talking about their dates and their chances to be models and singers. Mama says it's always better to have the kind of friends who tell you the truth than those who let you get into trouble with your eyes open. I wouldn't say I like talking about people behind their backs. I tell whatever is needed while my friends are with me. It's better to be honest with everyone.

Everyone comes into the world to be whatever they are supposed to be. Only God can change people, and if he sees them as a special kind of child, no one else can change that. Just love everyone and help make a better world. The world needs more love, not hate. It will never be the right way for human beings to live.

One day there will be hope for all the different people who want to help our world. God loves his creation and is happy to look down on the earth and see everyone singing, living, loving, and working to make a better world. I think it's fantastic to be of the human race and nothing less. It's great to have the ability to love another person and feel special. I love being on the earth that we are on. The things that we have now are incredible. We have green grass and trees and flowers of so many colors. We have pools to swim in and the sun to shine down on us. I love the way our world is, and I love having a chance to make life what it should be.

I know my sisters are different from me, and we are pleased about different tastes in styles. We can choose other clothes and hair, and I like that. My brother is different. He's a boy. My sisters have different tastes in the boys. The best way for people to be is to have exceptional tastes.

Mama tells me to stay as I am; she thinks my hair and face go perfectly together. Monde says it would be very boring to have everyone looking alike or having the same taste. Having the ability to think differently and having different ideas are the real things keeping us human beings making changes and creating the different shapes of tall skyscrapers and clothes. He says the movie stars wouldn't be special if they all look alike. He loves to talk about the science of life and human beings. Monde says cloning will be the biggest catastrophe ever made on earth. He says there would be massive confusion all the time.

Chapter Seven

THE TWIN LOOKS

The world would never be a place of happiness because everybody will be looking at identical places all the time and getting bored. People will always want to be different because of self-awareness. It helps people look at themselves before leaving the house each day.

I laugh and laugh at Monde. He is telling the truth, and he says everything with a serious face. He sometimes stops and laughs with me, but he says he sees the future most of the time. He wants me to listen before I laugh, but I can't help laughing because it sounds so funny. I believe Monde because if everybody looked the same, what would be the reason for getting up and choosing all the different clothes to wear or the different houses in which to live. Everyone would have the same mind, and nothing would make a difference. Children in our world today prefer to have their unique styles.

I would not like to be a teacher in a school where every other child looks the same or acts the same. It would be a place of total confusion all day. Monde is right, and he makes lots of sense to me most of the time. To tell the truth,

I'm scared about a lot of things. People around the world keep doing things that don't seem right.

There was a promotion one day at work when we gave away free french fries. All day long, the people kept coming. I thought I saw the same faces. They wore the same clothes, so I asked my coworkers if they saw people walk in that looked like those coming in that had left a minute ago. It turned out that they were experiencing the same thing, so we decided to keep a list of all the faces that came in looking exactly like the others.

That was an excellent idea because we found that over twenty people had come in with identical faces, hair, clothes, and even the same walk! We thought that maybe they were sent in by a scientist or somebody experimenting to see how much their new cloned people could eat or something like that. We never found out, but it was a pretty scary experience. It made me see what everybody has been saying about a messed-up world full of strange things going on.

Sometimes I wonder if the scientists will help change the world or keep practicing and become plain old bored with their ideas. Instead of thinking of ways to make more people, they should be thinking of ways to help the poor.

They should make sure the children could get good healthcare and always enough food worldwide. I don't believe children should suffer from a lack of food or anything because they are our future.

The brain is so powerful, and it can do anything it wants to do. I think about all the people who make music and about movie stars. They get rich quickly. They have everything they ever wanted because they can become great.

Mama says the folks who say terrible words to make children dance around and look silly aren't smart at all. I believe that someday, yes, some good old day on this earth, I'm going to succeed and be someone extraordinary, like a queen or a ruler of a big country.

Maybe I'll be an excellent singing star or something like that. Time will tell, and I'll keep believing in myself. I'm so glad I know what it takes to make it in this world. I'm waiting to march down the aisle to the sound of "Pop and Circumstance." My chances to be anything I want then will be a greater reality. I like to write about things that are happening around me. It all sounds so strange to me, like all forms of evil, but it's real everyday life in the world that a whole world of children and I recognize. I can't see what's so different about human needs because we all need to go to school and learn. We all need to live in a house and read good books. We all need to love, be loved, laugh, cry, eat, and play as we grow up and do all the things nature intended to function correctly. We must do all we can to help make the world a better place to live for the new children that come to life every day.

Mama keeps telling me, "Girl, if you stop worrying about the crazy things in the world, then maybe success will come sooner than you think." There is one thing that I keep learning every day, and that is forgetting about many of the negative things that happen helps them to soon go away from the mind and fade entirely away from you. It's like complete healing of the heart.

Since I keep learning about the mind in my health classes, I've learned many great things about life. It's wonderful to understand what is needed to be healthy and be careful to stay away from all the negative stuff. It's no way to get anything good from the negatives. I learned that in my chemistry class. I love learning, and I learn a lot in school. Sometimes I feel like writing the President or somebody and asking if they could come and see how much poor children can learn. I think the people of authority forget about the poor and refuse to get involved with critical issues. They don't know or care if we are learning. They stay so far away from the children, smaller cities, and schools. We need many new books and papers to get our work done because we like writing and learning new things.

Sometimes it seems like nobody cares. Children come into the world and are full of questions. They want to know about everything they see and don't understand, like the rain, snow, cumulus clouds, sun, flowers, trees, grass, fruits, vegetables, different tastes like sweet and sour, and how things grow on trees on earth. We all want to know more about the world, sand, seashells, fish in the sea, planet earth itself which is so big, different people everywhere, trains, airplanes, boats, and especially the foods we have to eat.

Children want to know all the stuff that seems complicated to figure out. I love my teachers. They have lots of experiments for the children in school. They are the best, and they use their money for the poor kids because we don't have money to buy everything needed.

The parents come up to the school to help the teachers. That's why I love my school. We are like a big family. Everybody knows your family, and the teachers are a part of that family.

Sometimes I walk the long way home and look up at the sky, and I thank God for making such a pretty world for us to live in, the sun, beautiful butterflies, and green grass to fall on and lay flat out. I laugh and laugh. Sometimes as I lay on that good-smelling grass. I promise God that I will do all I can to help His world stay beautiful.

Mama says it takes all kinds to help make up a universe of different types of folks. She says it gives people work to do every day because He sees everything all the time. I am confident that I'll never be able to handle the world and its troubles, but I instead want to try to make it a better place and have a chance to sing or dance and maybe be a teacher.

I can hear the sound of "Pomp and Circumstance" all in my head. I'm happy as can be. Monde says it doesn't matter if people get rich or not. He says all that matters is that people love their lives and do all they can to make the lives of their families and their own lives better. He is correct, but it takes lots of hard work since most people want a better life, they are glad to work. I will keep thinking about the possible chance to succeed in getting an excellent education.

I like to talk to my teachers about a lot of things. They want some of my ideas, and they tell me to keep working on the things that I have confidence in, like all the things that I think of as new ideas. They taught me most of the things I know. I love reading, writing, and English, and sometimes I like science. Monde says he loves science more than anything. He loves chemistry and English too.

Mama says there is not too much she can teach me, except how to be a nice, intelligent person and not to be silly around boys. She says they soon get tired of the silly girls. Most boys like to feel smart all the time.

Mama says the boys look for the smart girls to make them look good, and the girls encourage them to be good in their sports and books. I know because Monde and I tell each other all the good stuff to encourage each other.

I keep a smile because Mama says, "A happy face is always a nice face if you keep a smile. Even if it's a small one." I see people coming and going to work looking so angry, and they never smile back. I say, Millie, you got a great smile. I smile even if some look angry because it makes people feel better to get a smile. I think that I got to look different. It doesn't make sense to go around looking angry every day.

Like the changing seasons, people are different. I like being me and being nice most of the time. I can be fearful sometimes, but I'm happy that I know how to smile. When I see that I'm right about things, I keep fighting to make somebody understand what I'm trying to say. It sometimes is my Grandma, my Grandpa, or my teachers. But I get what I want if they listen. Mama says it's okay to ask somebody else about their opinions because it takes the minds of intelligent people to help out with complex problems.

I know that my questions and ideas can be huge at times. I can't bore Mama with everything all the time, so Monde is the best listener for me. Monde says I should give myself a rest from the world's problems. I laugh and laugh, and he starts laughing with me. He then says, "Millie, you can find all the answers inside you. There's so much knowledge in my head where no one can ever get in."

I feel my mind loves to think, and it's something that the mind needs. It's called an exercise of the brain. Imagining the tough things of life and the things that seem impossible gives the mind a lot of work, but I feel great after thinking and coming up with some answers. Maybe I don't have answers to everything, but it does not take long to figure things out. I think the best thing for the people to do is pray, be good to each other, and not let things get next to them all the time.

Smiling makes people look at you and start thinking about good things, and that's what makes life worth living, considering there are more good people in the world than bad. When I see the children at school with sad faces, I imagine what happened before leaving their house. I sometimes think that they may have fought with somebody, so I skip along, minding my own business unless they are a friend.

Some people are upset all the time, and I think maybe it's because they are mad at the world or something. One girl I know, Norda, doesn't let anybody ask or say anything to her before ten o'clock. She is very fussy and acts touch me not with everybody. But after ten o'clock has passed, she is the happiest child in the school. She starts talking with the other children, but they just stand and look at her, not knowing what to say because she is so mean to everybody before ten o'clock. She is very unpredictable. I think it's time for me to ask her some questions. If she comes my way, I look at her with my big happy smile to let her know everything is okay, and maybe she will have a good day. I will let her know it's okay to smile all the time. She would have more friends if she did. I think there's something wrong if people are angry all the time. I could be that way too, but Mama does all she can to keep us happy. She cares a lot about her children. I think I'll tell her someday, but not until I graduate. I can hear the sound of "Pomp and Circumstance" all in my head.

There's a student I know in school, Spanki, who gets so scared when the teacher asks questions. He tries to look mean, and he slides down into his seat and pokes his mouth out like the teacher had said something wrong about him. Maybe someday he'll take a good look at his face before leaving the house because he looks very nice when he's happy.

All the students want to walk or run from angry people all the time. It's not the way to have friends. Mama says, "A girl with a nice personality will grow up to be very special." She even says a person can get well if they look at a happy smile. Mama says, "A smile doesn't cost a cent, and it can significantly impact many people in one day." I get so glad listening to my Mama. Someday I want to help needy children everywhere.

Chapter Eight

MARCHING TOWARD THE BIG GOAL

It will soon be prom and graduation time, and things are getting better for me as I save my money up. So far, my bank account is growing. I can go to the best stores and buy my clothes for special times. I'm glad that I got Monde to take me to the prom because there are some girls at school running around still looking for a boy to take them out.

They have always dated anyone they wanted, and now it seems as though the boys have forgotten who they were. Those girls were always going out and dating before they were supposed to. The boy said he wants a new girl to date on their special night. It is a shame to date the guy all the time. Then he looks for a new person to take to the prom. Girls have a lot of terrible lessons to learn while growing up.

I wish I knew the answers to most things that seem so strange and so out of order. I think about a lot of things all the time, but now it's time for me to think about the good stuff only.

Before I became a senior, I used to look in the mirror all the time. I would wonder how I looked to the world. I never had a true sense of self or being beautiful after the horrible thing that happened to me. That's why I love Mama. She always says I look gorgeous no matter what I wear. So, I go on to school happy, like I was the richest girl in town. Now I say to my little sister to never worry about what people say, be happy about who she is, and try to stay little as long as she can. I tell her not to grow up too early and wait for time to get what nature wants to give her. For now, I'll be quiet and accept myself wholeheartedly. I'll never worry about my size and shape. I think more about getting perfect grades because I know some of the evils in this world.

I feel good growing up and learning how to be the best I can be. Monde is like a big brother and part of the family now. He likes to eat Mama's food. I'm happy to know that I'm very near my first big goal.

My Mama can be so funny. Today she looked at me walking into the house with an armload of books. She said I was carrying too many. She says girls should be careful carrying a big heavy load of anything. I laugh and tell her, "I got to have all those books because it's time to graduate soon, and I have to pass all my tests." I can hear the sound of "Pomp and Circumstance" all in my head! Then she says, "Girl, you know you will pass the tests because you got enough brains to share with the whole world." I laugh, and she laughs, saying she was proud of me with all the sense I got. It makes me feel so good to listen to my Mama. She tells me a lot of stuff. I tell Mama I want a better education than the one she got. She says I'm right. It makes her feel happy to know her children will be successful in life.

One other thing she tells me is that I have to be more than book smart. She says it's important to be naturally bright too. She says that I have to know the basic things about life and everyday survival. I keep listening to her because she knows a lot about the real way of life.

Chapter Nine

LOOKING AT THE INSIDE

While getting dressed for school this morning, I saw my Mama stop working and stand with her hands on her hips. Then she says, "Miss lady, you need to get out of the mirror and stop putting on all that." I laugh and say, "It's only a free giveaway from the store. I'm trying it out for now. I know I don't need it."

My Mama laughed and laughed. She laughed so hard she had to go to her chair and sit down. That's the way it is around my house. Whether it's in the morning or late at night, we always have time for good laughter. After laughing with my Mama, I saw most of my makeup had come off, so I walked right back into the bathroom to put some more on. Just not as much as before because Mama is always right. She wants me to look right when I go out into the universe. She looks over all her children before we walk out of her house.

When she looks at me, she says, you look all right for a little teenage girl, and you pass the test. Now go on to school and get a couple more A's and B's. I say to her I will settle for the A's only.

I feel pretty most times, but being like the movie stars is hard work. I'm still waiting to get all the best of everything. It's important to be the best you can be. When I think I need to be funny about things, my Mama tells me to stop it and be grateful. She said it in a fussing voice because she can be upset with me sometimes. When I think a pimple or something is looking bad, Mama makes me see it's not all bad after all.

She doesn't fuss that much, but it makes all the sense in the world whenever she does. It makes you see better than before. It's good sound advice. Whatever Mama says, she knows that on the inside of me, there's a nice person who has a good heart and lots of good ideas to help save the world. The way my Mama sits around and looks out the window is a little funny. I tell her sometimes she should go for walks or something, and then suddenly, she makes a lot of sense because that is what she wants to do.

A lot is going on in the world, and she likes to get the feel of things before she decides which direction to go. That makes a lot of sense to me. You have to take care of yourself. She and her friends know who lives where, and sometimes they pick up the phone and call each other to tell them to look out the window at the person in a beautiful hat or some strange looks or something. Like I said before, those women tickle me crazy. They talk for long hours about what they see coming down the street.

It pays to know who lives next door to you, but Mama and I disagree about looking out the window at everybody coming and going. Monde says it's right in some ways, especially when they are lonely or something, and it helps them think about something. My Mama isn't lonely. She always needs to know everything.

Sometimes she and her friends go places together. They like to shop for foods on sale and go out to have their hair done and lunch sometimes. They share unique recipes. To tell the truth, I would be rather bored if it was not for my Mama and her friends. It's an absolute pleasure.

I love my Mama. She is all I will ever have, and there will never be another like her. I'm still waiting to be like her in my heart because she is so special. Everything I talk about, she already knows. She can tell me how to deal with life. She tells me a lot about hair and the suitable styles to wear. Mama used to do hair when she was young, but she says the chemicals got too much for her to inhale. She can make some pretty clothes when she feels like sewing. She can cook real good, and her food tastes a whole lot better than restaurants. I learned to be careful about eating foods that don't seem right at first sight.

It takes a lot of wisdom to live in a great big world. God is everywhere, so for that reason, no one should worry. Today, I wore a beautiful pink outfit with a scarf that matches. My friends liked it and complimented me. They asked where I bought it, and you know what? I was the proudest girl in the world because it was the first time I ever had a gift from a boy. It was a birthday gift from Monde. I was a proud senior. I can hear the sound of "Pomp and Circumstance" all in my head!

It was the best time of my life to become a senior. We had lots of meetings and lots of fun places to go. We are buying our prom and senior luncheon clothes. Mama wants to make my prom dress, but I keep looking at this fabulous dress in the window of one of the popular stores. It doesn't cost that much, and at this time, I have saved up enough money to buy whatever I need to look like a princess for the best day of my life.

You know something. I have learned to keep my business to myself because I can see how terrible jealousy works in people. I see the way their eyes watch you when you wear something pretty and walk like a real lady. The faces of some of the girls are scary sometimes. I don't have time for them. I'm just too far ahead of jealousy and being evil. By the time I get out of college, I'll have even more things in my mind to do and achieve before a certain age. Jealousy will hold some people back. I heard Grandma and Mama say many things happen to people worldwide.

My teacher had a good long talk with the class today. She wanted to know about our future plans and what we want to be when we get out of college. A student acted like he didn't know what the teacher was talking about when the teacher asked for his homework, and this child is never on time. Sometimes they have the lesson, and sometimes they don't.

Teachers love to see well-cared-for children. Girls love the boys who act like they are somebody. They are the ones we admire.

A lot of children never learned how to respect themselves or their parents. It is sad to see a young student become a disgruntled human being early in life. They sometimes affect their life it by not listening to their families and teachers. The teachers are like mothers, and they are like family. Though no one else cares, they come to work every day to teach us and make us better human beings. All it takes is listening and doing the work because education is essential. I'm still waiting to march down the aisle to the incredible sound of "Pomp and Circumstance."

Chapter Ten

MILLIE'S IDEAS

Monde and I keep talking and sharing our ideas. We know a lot about things, and we do much research to find answers to things puzzling us. We think someday we can be very prosperous with good ideas, but I say that's okay as long as we develop something that will make a better world. We go to the library more than anybody I know on the planet. That's our regular meeting place, and it's our secret. Most of the students see us studying. They sit with us, but a lot of students don't even come to the library.

We saw people from all over at Sassie's birthday party. We found out that she had some important people present. Some of them were from the neighborhood youth center and theater. That night was special for all of us. I'll tell you why most of the students from my high school take theater classes. They want to be in the movies and be like all the rest of the stars and famous people someday.

The happiest children at the party were those expecting to become famous. The people from the theater told us they were looking for people with a lot of confidence in being great in theater and had a couple of thousand dollar prizes for the three of the best theater and dance students. That was the best news for everybody to hear, especially those who think they are already number one.

The best treat at her party was to surprise everybody with a popular singing group. Suddenly, the dance group came walking through the door to surprise Sassie. The girl is great at doing funny stuff. She keeps us laughing. Since she knows everybody and thinks she is the best actress on earth, I think so too. The girl is funny. She isn't ashamed that she comes from a low-income family. She always says it was the road she had to travel to get where she has to be in life. Her oldest sister knows the singing group, and it was easy for her to get the favor from them to surprise Sassie. They lived in the neighborhood before they got popular. They say they have to be positive role models for all kids because most kids don't have a daddy. They are glad to have the dance group to be able to take time out for them in the after-school programs. Every day they run back and forth to school like they are the happiest kids on earth. It's great to have special folks come around when you're little; we looked forward to them.

It was kind of funny when two of the dancers started taking the floor. They danced and danced until everybody else moved back and let them have the floor. They thought they were the best in the house. That was okay, but they acted like they wanted all the attention. Monde and I just sat down and waited for them to finish their dance. They decided to keep the floor. We thought they would never quit, so Monde, some other kids. and I just got up on our favorite song and started dancing. We were rather pitiful, but we still know how to dance with rhythm, you know. The best dancers never stopped, they just danced the night away, and when all the rest of us got up and started dancing, they looked at us as if we were supposed to sit and watch them.

That was not how the party was going to end, and we all knew that it was a fair and square dance party. The singing group New Daze performed one more of their popular songs and left. We were the happiest kids that night. The dance troupe who thought they were the best figured we would get out of the way again, but everybody just kept dancing. They said they want to be seen by the group too and that it wasn't fair to let the other people take over. We just laughed and laughed. It was so funny to see their faces.

The real winners of the dance were the couple who everybody knew as the top dancers during our high school parties. They were the best. One good thing for Sassie was that she finally got herself straight because she was one bad little girl at one time. She didn't care, and she ran around with all the bad kids. She and two others won the theater prize. Sassie never forgot the time she was out too late, and they were all taken to the police station. Sassie was so scared of her mama maybe putting her out that she ran away from home. That worried everybody that knew the family. She was at a friend's house for weeks. Eventually, her older sister found her, took her back home, asked her to stay out of trouble, and promised to do something special for her birthday. From that day on, Sassie stayed out of trouble.

Everybody always said something good about her. The girl was smart. She grew up on a forgotten side of town, and it wasn't much she could do about that. The people said she was one poor little girl who walked around the town with her head held high. Even when she didn't have her hair combed, she was proud. She said she knew she was extraordinary even then.

Some people never forget anything about you. They sit around and talk about you even when you think you are off their gossip list. To tell the truth, it's a list that never fades away. They reach back into their heads and bring up the past whenever they are bored of talking about the folks on the top of their gossip list. My Mama always says, "Try to be nice every day of your life because the people watch you and talk. If it's good or bad, they still talk." Sometimes I feel proud to be slower when it comes to living in the fast lane. I prefer to live a healthy life rather than an unhealthy lifestyle.

It's the right way to be since I finally have a good friend like Monde. We both are the same kind of people. We like the same things and think the same things. We know we have to have a good education to get most jobs. I can hear the sound of "Pomp and Circumstance" in my head.

When I think about being grown, he tells me to slow down. I laugh and laugh since Monde doesn't know how important it is to me. Since I have to wait, I guess that's what I must do, but I will keep thinking about a big house and all my dream things. I hope someday to get all the stuff on my grown-up list. I think my list would reach the north pole and back, and I still have new stuff to add to the list. I'm still waiting to grow up and have the best life and the best education—most of all, the best vacations that I could have. I'm still waiting.

Now that winter has left and spring has come, I get up early. I love making my breakfast. Mama says after I graduate, she will let me do all the cooking I want to do since I will be almost on my own. Mama is so funny. She makes me laugh till I fall to the floor. I'm not kidding.

Chapter Eleven

SITTING AND LAUGHING WITH MAMA

Mama loves to sit and look out the window, no matter what kind of weather it is. She sits in the summer, spring, fall, and winter. Even when the snow fills the windowsills, she sits and looks at all the snow and says funny stuff like the snow is so white I can't even see the sky. I tell her that it's snowing and it is supposed to look that way. We laugh and laugh. She knows how to get me involved in her pastime pleasure even though I tell her how silly it looks.

When I get ready early, while waiting for Monde, I grab my chair and sit with her. We sit back to back, looking out at the sunshine, fog, rain, and snow. Watching people can be fascinating. Now I must say, I don't talk about the folks like Mama and her friends because I do have a life. Sitting back to back with Mama like two knots on a log can be the best way for me to wait for my friend Monde, and it relaxes me. We look so silly sitting there telling each other what we see from our site. Some bizarre things are going on outside and passing by the windows. You might laugh yourself silly.

I get up and fix us a good snack, cheese and crackers, sometimes mixed fruits with whipped cream on top, or peanut butter and jelly sandwiches. Whatever I make, Mama always calls it my special gourmet platter.

I start laughing all over again because it is nowhere near the gourmet foods I want to experience in the future. Mama says it's all she has to do most times, and it gives her something to ponder. It does help me stop worrying, especially if it's something unnecessary. When I was little, I used to sit with Mama. It was lots of fun but not so much now. It helps me pass the time away. The funny thing about the window sitting now is that she sits and looks north, and I sit and look south. That's very funny to Monde. He wonders how anybody can sit all day and look at the same things. I tell him nothing is the same because the view changes. That's what Mama likes about her pastime hobby.

When Monde comes to take me to the library, I wave to him, and he tells me to say hello to Mama. I get my hat and coat and go downstairs to meet him. He and Mama like each other very much. He always sends her candy and pretty little gifts. I think that's an excellent idea because she deserves all the good things. My Mama loves everybody's children. She always lets them stay over when they don't know to go home. When she babysits them, she says that they are the best little human beings in the world. They need the right people to raise them.

My Mama is right. She is hardly anything else but right, and I trust what she says. When I was little, I didn't do what she said about wearing my snow boots and my long underwear. I would get so cold and almost freeze. I knew then that Mama was always right, and I learned to listen to her.

I think the world is changing fast. Monde says the year 2000 will be very different from the century before it. He says clothes will start to look different in the 21st century, but the people will stay the same. I promised Monde I would not change. No matter what the people do, he says he will remain the same. For now, we will keep thinking about getting a better education than our parents. I can hear the sound of "Pomp and Circumstance."

Our lifestyles will change, and we will be very successful. As president of my senior class, I'm a role model, and I try to dress right. Monde reminds me to wear scarves in case the weather changes.

Chapter Twelve

MILLIE'S SHOCKING EXPERIENCE

That's what makes Mama love him so. He acts like a doctor already. She says he is too intelligent for his age. I'm not too fond of scarves. I think they make me look older than I am, and Mama hates to see me walk outside without one after the cold weather sets in, so I guess I'll be taken care of pretty well with Monde acting like a doctor. I want to be healthy and wise, and taking care of myself is a good start. After all, role models have to act and dress the part. I think girls and boys should be neat and clean every day, but boys can get away with a lot more things than girls. You know what? The whole world seems to see it like that. I think it's because the boys and men have to do the real rugged work in life like building the tall skyscrapers and the homes where we live. I'm glad we can all be doctors, teachers, and scientists though.

Sometimes Mama likes to start stuff with Monde and me. She asks Monde about the foods he likes to eat. Then she tells him my way of cooking is something he would like. I wait to see what he was going to say, and then I give him a google-eyed look like he may need to think before commenting on such a touchy conversation like that. Then suddenly, the room is full of hearty laughter. Mama has a terrific laugh and says that's one of the greatest gifts of life.

Then it's my time to brag about all the good cookies I make and some of the favorite dishes they like, especially for the holidays. Mama has another good laugh and says, "I love your food, baby, and you keep cooking for your Mama now." Nothing can shake my confidence. I'm artistic, and cooking is just another form of art.

I proudly say how hard I try to encourage the students of our time as it is. We must learn how to get along with each other, fight evil, and learn to understand and communicate with the many different cultures. We must have a decent world for children to come into—a world that's full of love. Mama and Monde agree with me and say somebody has to do it. I say it might as well be good ole Millie. We all laugh at that because the job is not for one person. It takes a village or city of real concerned human beings. That's what I think, and I think a whole lot of people feel like me. It's just a significant big problem that has been going on for too long.

I think when our high school luncheon, prom, and graduation come around, I might feel like a grown-up a little bit. I have many things on my mind about the world, life, and college, and it sometimes gives me a feeling of being grown already. I'm telling you the truth.

One thing Mama keeps saying is that I should stop worrying about the world, take one day at a time, and live my young life like it's the only one I'll ever have. That makes me laugh. I think it's the only chance to be a young lady and that I'm going to try my best to be patient with the world getting better for all the children on the way and all the people suffering through life every day.

To hear my Mama talk about life will scare a girl not taught much. She says it's a shame for children to drop out of school early because their life will be a real mess. They'll have nothing to do but sit around the house feeling left out and useless. Most times, they stare out the window at all the other children going to school. And the girls will wish they could look pretty like all the others that pass by.

Mama knows what she's talking about because life was pretty tough for her as a young woman, but she says she doesn't have too many regrets because we made her life complete. She says she's had some excellent times too. When she got married, Mama was glad to stay home, have her children, and be a good mother for us. She says it was fun to learn all about little human beings and enjoy the baby's first words.

Our first day in school, where we would learn the things that will help us be smart and be very educated, was her happiest since it would make us better educated than her. I'm proud of my Mama. She went to work and made her life better. Mama does what she feels is her calling, helping the older people, and she enjoys going places with her friends when she's off work. She's a smart lady and the real inspiration in my life. Mama says she can see that Monde and I will be perfect friends. He is so kind and polite. He knows how to talk to her and people from all walks of life.

I guess that's why he became a supervisor at an early age and why people like him for being an outstanding business person. I feel I can trust him to be real all the time. I feel exceptional to know such a wonderful human being as Monde. Both of us believe in thinking. We are possible future leaders and hopefully great ones.

Sometimes we even believe it may be the two of us who will help change the world. That's when Mama has a good laugh. She says she would love to see two young people do something as extraordinary as that. Mama says she would be so proud to have one of her children do what she used to dream of doing.

Mama loves to listen to us sit around and talk about things. She had fun fixing us big plates of her excellent food and lemonade. She asks many questions and waits for us to answer them one at a time, and she almost falls to the floor laughing at the stuff we tell her. We like to talk about the crazy things that happen outside and at work. She says she can't believe the things we say.

The phone rang, and Millie answered. It was the mother of the two children she babysits. The mother asked Millie to come over and watch the children for the evening because she wanted to go out to dinner with her friends. For Millie, this was just fine because she could use the extra money for her new clothes. Millie let her mom know about the call for her to babysit and changing clothes if she was staying all night, as she often does. It was only a block away from her house. As she walked down Cedar Street, she could only think about all the beautiful clothes and shoes she would purchase for the different occasions and the graduation fees to pay.

Millie arrived, and the mom greeted her happily. Her mother let her know where to call if needed and instructed her about the needs of the children. The pizza was to be delivered. The oldest, a girl, age seven, and a boy, age five, were never any trouble. They loved Millie as if she was their big sister.

The children, Lian and Mishawn, are always delighted to have Millie babysit them. Before the mother left, they were on the couch listening to Millie read a book from one of the stacks of books; her mother told her to choose from one of the stacks of books. The evening was going fast because they were enjoying each other. Millie took the little girl to her room to get into her pajamas, and that's when the door opened abruptly. Holding a bag in one hand, Mr. Thomas, the children's father, motioned to his daughter to leave the room with the other hand. Millie was startled because she did not know what was about to happen. She jumped in surprise, asking what it was that he wanted. He seemed shocked to see her as if he didn't know she was there.

Holding the bag in his hand, he walked over to the closet while thinking of a place to attack her, but instead, he laid the bag down. Millie was thinking about the traumatic experience she dealt with at the age of five. In a moment, she remembered every detail of that horrible day. Millie remembered his voice, look, and smell and prayed to God not to let it happen again. Millie thought about what she heard from different girls that never overcame the horrors of being raped. She could only think of finding a way to escape or fight back. A teenager molested Millie at five years old. She never told her mother what happened. He had warned her that he would kill everybody in her family if she ever said a word. Another brilliant child with great potential was stripped of the real chance to grow up as an average-thinking child, forcing her to know the one evil that made fear a reality. Millie thought of the self-defense and karate classes she had taken. All the techniques and ways to fight back flashed through her mind. She was ready for anything, she thought. I'm not afraid. I am not scared—repeating it over and over again.

Before Millie could explain, he advanced toward her, reaching for her arm as though he was about to attack her. Speaking forcefully, he ordered his daughter to go back to the front room to sit with her brother. At this time, Millie was very frightened and asked what did he want from her. He spoke with a quiet voice, asking her to stay low-key. Millie was thinking of a way to escape. She noticed that his eyes were on her, looking like there was no way out of the room.

"Please don't hurt me," she begged. He said, "Millie, why are you so frightened? I came by to leave this gift for Lian. Tomorrow is her birthday. It's the laptop she always wanted." Millie relaxed and sat down on the bed, holding her hands together. She said, "Oh my! I forgot about her birthday. I'm sorry to have acted startled, Mr. Thomas. I'm

not used to anyone coming into the room when I babysit."
He said, "Oh, that's okay, Millie, you are a great young lady,
and thanks for watching the children. Make sure Lian
doesn't see the gift until tomorrow. Her mom knows about
it." Millie said, "No problem, I will make sure it stays hidden
from her."

Millie thought about the close call and that it could have
been the horror she felt it was, but she was again one of the
happiest girls on earth. She looked up to pray and thank God
for protecting her.

Chapter Thirteen

MILLE'S GIFT FOR MAMA

Mama is careful about going into too many unfamiliar places. Her job takes her to excellent restaurants. She and her friends choose good places to go and shop for their dainty little things, like perfume and lingerie. I like to give thanks for the new stuff I can buy, and for some reason, I know that a lot of beautiful things are waiting for me. I just got to wait until after my graduation before I start spending. Gee whiz! I'm so happy. I can hear the sound of "Pomp and Circumstance."

It's going to be great to hold that diploma in my hand, and I'm going to shout out Hallelujah! I'll be on my way to college from there, and I can see the new and exciting life ahead of me. Mama says she's more excited than me. I'll be the second child of hers to graduate. Monee will graduate next year, and she has already chosen her college. I'm proud of my big sister.

My job is not paying me a real big salary because I haven't worked as a full-time employee yet, but the amount is perfect. It allows me to save and get the essential things, like clothes and school books.

After a certain girl came to school telling everybody about her dress last year, the whole senior class was excited! The word got around, and the talk was out. Girls started looking for jobs like mad, and the guys didn't have many weekend dates then. They had no choice but to study for their big tests and get high scores.

Yes, the national exam scores for the school did improve. The girls decided to get jobs instead of socializing. They wanted to look as pretty as the next girl at that special time of her life. I tell them they are beautiful just as they are. Sometimes they look at me, and I ask if I'm honest with them. That's when we have a nice long talk about believing in ourselves. Every girl needs a mom like mine, one who looks after them and tells them how beautiful they are all the time.

This positivity helps build up self-work, and it will stay in her mind when the parents say it often. A girl won't have to stay in a mirror all the time then because she will know she's beautiful, even after swimming in the pool and the wind that blows it all over her head. Self-esteem is all a person needs. It allows a unique faith to live within. I have little savings, and after graduation, I will start college and looking to a great future. I think clothes should not cost too much. After all, they will soon get old. You lose interest in wearing them, and then you give them away. My favorite clothes are denim pants, skirts, and long slinky skirts. They feel good on me, and they look nice wherever I go in them.

Mama says she loves the way I match up all my clothes. I laugh and tell her I don't have that much trouble because mostly everything is denim and simple skirts and tops. I try to match my shoes with most of my everyday clothes. I love shoes. When I first start working, that was the first thing that I bought. Shoes were always challenging for Mama to buy. She had three other children to buy for, and it wasn't easy to have many of the most important things that children want.

Today I feel like a very successful teenager because while in high school, there were so many new experiences with people of all ages and cultures. I say to myself, Millie, you are so different from the way you used to be. I think, yes, all because I grew up and learned how to use my mind to move past the things that tried to stop my thinking, especially the creative skills, like the beautiful art I learned as a child. I would love to make my paper dolls and cut out beautiful clothes from the catalogs. I desire to be a fashion model because I like all the pretty clothes they wear. It seems strange now because I want to get the clothes and wear them. I still create beautiful paintings in my art classes. I get all A's because it's one of my favorite classes.

My teachers know me for passing all my tests, and that's a great feeling. I know life has specific things to experience, but the lesson is so different for each human being. One of the great things I will do in life is teaching children and parents to love one another as God asks of us. I feel energized just saying the word love. Since I have a strong Mama, I think challenges came to show me how to stand up and keep walking tall. Children are born to experience a better world than their parents. Most parents want this for their children.

Some parents know how important it is to ensure that children are in the proper environments and protect them from hostile forces. Mothers and fathers are the first teachers and should be the best influence in the child's life. It helps build great self-esteem, and children grow up healthy and happier. I think like this because of some of the children I babysit. They come home talking about all the mean people and the mean faces they see all day long. Well, that's not good for children to go through every day of their early years. It only teaches them to become hostile, and they'll lack social skills as they grow up. Children learn about fear and anger from the people around them. It would better for parents to stay home with their children while they are small.

It will make both parent and child happier. I'm not sure why I know all this. I just know.

I am selected to speak at my graduation ceremony. Though it's a month before graduation, I feel the excitement and fulfillment of being the valedictorian of my graduation class. I can hear the sound of "Pomp and Circumstance" all in my head! I get goosebumps when I write about the need for graduates to be good examples by striving for the highest goals and showing respect for each other. I will explain the need to understand the power of unity, goals, and dreams and a great determination to make a better world.

I will speak on the need to seek ways to make a difference as we advance to each new class, group, and educational level. I'm grateful for my opportunity to have friends of every culture. We ate together, studied together, and played together. Therefore, I can honestly ask, are we different? I have my answer for now. It will be the key to opening every door that I desire to walk through. I will be prepared to find answers, even if popular opinions says there isn't a way. I will tell them I need to equip them for a fast-paced world, know their skills and abilities, and not settle for the word no. As of now, I have very little time to waste. I must use every minute thinking of a speech that my peers will remember.

Monde called to share some information about great speakers. He meets great people all the time. I will need some ideas for my speech. Maybe he will share his speech as well. Sometimes he prefers to remain secret about important things. That's okay. It's a crucial moment for both of us, and Mama always says never tell too much of your business. I believe there is excellent work for Monde and me.

I have to wait and see. For now, I'm so happy to know Monde as a great friend. We do our homework together sometimes. He called and told me that one of his former teachers would attend the graduation. He was greatly surprised. The first time was when they called a few weeks ago requesting his presence to speak at my graduation. Monde said he accepted with lots of gratitude. He said this is his first time invited to return as a speaker since being valedictorian two years ago.

He said it's a great honor. For me, it was exciting and out of this world to know we both share encouraging information with the students. We will both seek the right words to say to the future leaders of our world. Since he is now a sophomore in college, he's proud to tell his friends.

Monde said he would try and give the students the information to help them get through their first year and the next three depending on if they wanted to go to the highest levels. Monde said we all need good mentors to help make it through life. He said that high school is one of the most important times to have good tutors and mentors and that the college years are significant.

I will let them know that we have succeeded as a community at a vital time in life and that our years of bonding are the key to a lifetime of connecting and successful growth. I will remain as a girl thinking she has the most answers in my speech but not forcing her opinions on anyone. Therefore, my actual point and message to the graduating class will be to paint the picture, hard work, less partying, and more devotion to research and library visits. I will inform them of the mental and spiritual fortitude existing deep within the soul in my speech. Also, there is the need to demonstrate and use every gift God has given us while still young and have insights into the normal aspects of life. I will stress to them the need to be well-disciplined in life.

I will say that we have advanced from small children to adolescents with many roads to travel. We will soon have to make big decisions that could determine our families and lives. We are essential not only to ourselves but to the entire universe. The students, designed for this day and time, have determination and faith in themselves. They will arrive. I will remind the students that we must remember the legacy of great leaders such as W. E. B. Du Bois, Booker T. Washington, and Martin Luther King, Jr. They remind us of the importance of having a dream, holding on, and never giving up.

I'm so proud of Monde. He is an intelligent person. Most people say that about him, but he doesn't let all the good talk get to his head. He says his mama taught him to stay the same and not get too excited about all the fan club members. He said his mind is supposed to stay regular, not stuck up and acting like he's more than everybody else. I agree with him about being normal because sometimes people let things change them after they get famous.

Monde doesn't think he's all that famous or anything, but he does know that he has a lot of good information in his head, and he is glad to share his thoughts with my graduating class. I get goosebumps thinking about talking to a smart person.

I know how hard it was for me to think that I would have a lovely new friend. But when I found my job, I met my new friend Monde, and he is very nice. We have to grow up sometime, so it only fits the little children to have a chance. I think the whole world should be asking questions, and most important of all, they should try to find out how to teach about love and human feelings. Love helps children grow up to be kind, confident, and happy.

Children need listening to and some concern about their teachers and the type of day they had. I told Monde he should talk to the parents about this. He said he would say a little. Most of his speech will encourage the seniors never to stop studying and moving toward their goals.

Mama says I can talk about a lot of serious stuff, and maybe someday I will be invited to speak at different places like Monde. I say yes to that because I have a lot to say. My mind stays so full most of the time. I should go on a nice long vacation after graduation.

My Mama says I can go anywhere I want, for at least a week since I work. I laugh and laugh, and then she laughs with me because she knows where I work and that there aren't many people going on vacations there. One day in my future, I can and will go anywhere I want. I have to get my degrees. I can hear the sound of "Pomp and Circumstance" all in my head!

Graduation is very close, and this girl is so happy. I can hardly sleep at night. Mama asked if I want to get married someday soon. I tell her no and that I'll think about it after getting all my degrees. Then Mama says, "Well, that was a perfect answer, Millie, and whatever you think will be alright with me."

Monde looked at me and smiled with his mouth full of banana cream pie and cold milk. Mama feeds him so. He might get fat before I ever get a chance to bake some of the excellent cookie recipes she taught me. So, I say to her," Please don't give him any more of that banana cream pie."

Monde looked at me like I said a bad word because he was about to put his plate out for some more. I feel this way because he's my tutor, and I need him to stay healthy. Mama says he can take the whole thing home if he wants to.

I almost fell on the floor laughing. I asked my Mama, "Please don't give the whole thing to Monde. Can't you see how full he looks?" She said, "No, because a man should have all the food he wants, and a woman should be ready to give him as much as it takes to keep him happy as long as it's healthy for him."

Mama looked at Monde and smiled saying, "Don't let Millie tell you when to stop eating. Son, you the man. Her stomach is supposed to be smaller than a man's." Monde agreed with Mama. To tell the truth, he agrees with Mama about almost everything. Monde said he might learn to eat oatmeal eventually because he didn't like it that much when he was little. Now that Monde is older, he tries harder. We laugh and laugh. He can be so funny. Mama loves making him laugh, so we can have a pretty good time talking, eating, and laughing between the three of us. We live in a relatively small town of about three thousand people. That's about it.

Chapter Fourteen

MILLIE REACHES HER BIG GOAL

Everybody knows everybody's business in our town, but Monde and I say we're going to give only good things to say about us. Some wonder who the extra young man is that visits us, and they find out he's my tutor. Mama always says to live a quiet life and do all the good you can. I've learned a whole lot from my Mama. She's the best teacher I could have ever have. My favorite teacher, Ms. Irene Porter, was the best next to Mama. They taught me so well. I only wanted to see A's and B's on my grade cards.

Someday I will teach school and be as nice and understanding with students. It takes a good teacher to make good schools and students better. I'm proud to be who I am. With the mother I have and my family, life will be great. I will make my Mama the happiest woman on earth someday. But for now, it will be to receive my graduation certificate, one of her greatest gifts from me. Gee whiz! I can hear the sound of "Pomp and Circumstance" all in my head! Someday soon, I plan to send her on a couple of cruises and wherever she wants to go. Mama and her friend Ms. Baker are the two most caring people in the neighborhood. They now watch for the police since they love sitting at the window so much.

Today I give my Mama a soft chair pillow that I made in my art class. She was so happy, and she will use it for her special window chair. We had the best laugh. I was in tears.

Word got out about them seeing everything, and now they get a small pay for actually being on watch duty. They love their new jobs. The good thing about it is they are on their clock. They are the funniest people on the block. She and Ms. Baker have been good friends for as long as I can remember. They are always there for each other.

Monde says they should go on a cruise together since they have struggled in life. I agree with Monde and say, "Yes, they should go together and have the time of their life." That gift will come very soon. The two are very healthy and look great for their age. After watching Mama, I learned to care more about myself and do all I can to stay healthy. I hope I'll be as good as Mama someday, especially now that I'm on my way to college.

If we don't care about ourselves, we can't care much about life. God made me happy on this earth. It doesn't take a lot of money for children to grow up happy. Mama taught all her children to be good listeners, get along with each other, and love each other. What she taught us allows us to go out into the universe and love others.

There were hard times for us. We'll never forget most of it, but we will not remember some of it for our good. I think the main memories we should hold are sometimes those that go away until a sister or brother reminds you of it. And that's because someone has to provide the historical information of a family. But today, I will graduate! There will never be anything so wonderful as graduation. We have practiced for the march, and I got a taste of what the real moment will be like when it happens. As I write in my diary, I cannot forget to spell out great words of hope and an irresistible determination to acquire the best education and the best world possible. I understand it's not where I was born, live, or educated; it's all about the determination of an individual. In today's world, children are learning to eat healthy food. They learn more about nutrition and read labels while shopping with their parents.

Today is Millie's big day. She has chosen a beautiful pink dress with a sky blue collar and a matching blue ribbon belt. For a short while, she will be wearing her graduation gown. She can't wait to have pictures taken. The best part of it all is that she graduates with honors and is valedictorian of her class. As she hears her name called to speak, she sends her mom and family a great big smile, takes a good breath, and begins to talk.

To my classmates, teachers, parents, and friends, I realize that the one true source of my growth and staying power comes from God, my creator. I must give sincere thanks and heartfelt gratitude to my mother, grandparents, friends, and most of all, every teacher who shared precious time and energy to teach and correct me when they noticed I was not at my best. I now truly understand that it's not how little a child has in material goods, but in the love and warmth one feels from the people who mean the most.

Remember that you are unique. Refuse to be judged by the context of your skin. Know your self-worth, and stay determined to be the first to discover an answer to wipe out harmful disease, wars, and hunger. Use the gifts within you to invent new ways to save lives. As you advance toward the higher level of intellect, determine to use time wisely, for it is in knowing the true value of time that allows one to reap the greater benefits of its use. Some will become great physicians, educators, technicians, engineers, scientists, artists, musicians, and inventors. You are unique and extra special in more ways than imagined.

Therefore, my fellow graduates, I wish you the best life that lies beneath our great Heaven. I want for you the same simple hope I have for myself, that you strive with the dream in mind, with a clear focus on your goals and aspirations, no matter how hard it seems to get. But remember, when moments of disparity interrupt your life, be your motivator. Often the people we desire to talk with are nowhere to be found. Therefore, keep in mind these words. Never give up! The dreams and goals you have are only a hand-touch away. Time will allow you to walk right into the desires of your heart.

May you reach the unreachable stars, where your every dream comes true. I speak into your life the courage, confidence, faith, and determination to always have the spirit and willpower to achieve your desired goals. I know that there is nothing impossible with God. Understand that self-worth is what you think of yourself and that self-esteem allows you to continue believing in yourself. They both are different requirements for you to rise to your desired place of self-satisfaction as an individual in today's world. I refuse to be judged, denied, passed over, stigmatized, pushed aside, or neglected because of the context of my skin but to be accepted in any of my life's facets by my character.

I, Millie Reddington, will always demand the rights of which I was born and to have the freedom of human dignity and pride. I will be satisfied knowing that if the positions, places, and desires in life were not achieved, it was only due to my lack of hard work and determination and nothing less.

Regardless of your race, creed, or religion, classmates never allow anyone to judge you due to their opinions or fear of a true challenge. Make sure you have at least a fair chance to prove your self-work. It's your God-given right. And make sure you have accepted the knowledge and wisdom instilled within from the people who demonstrated concern and dedication to the exchange of knowledge. Your parents and teachers are who paved the way for you. Best wishes and may success and happiness forever be yours.

Today I have achieved the one most important goal for now. I have marched down the aisle with my classmates. I can't explain the feeling. I know that life will only get better. I've marched to the most important beat and musical arrangement. The sound of "Pomp and Circumstance" is no longer in my head. It's now a reality, and I will continue to work hard until I have every degree that satisfies my heart.

In signing out of my diary, I can say that my classmates enjoyed the speech. And it was greatly appreciated by all. I have come to experience the true feeling of self-worth as a colored girl in America.

No one cannot define the feeling I possess at this moment. One thing for sure, this girl named Millie Redington is well prepared for a life of nothing but the best. This world has everything for anybody who believes. I have learned what it takes to have a sound mind and a good heart. It makes a difference to help the less fortunate of the world in even the slightest way. I'm glad I grew up sitting by the window on occasion with Mama. I learned an awful lot.

I know it's all kinds of people in the world and that everybody has a way of surviving and making life work for them. I see the real world as it is, and most people live their best life with the knowledge and wisdom they have received. One thing I know for sure, that my struggle to live has been worthwhile and that nothing can compare to the day of unbelievable joy and happiness when reaching just one desired goal. It's unexplainable! One other important thing for everyone waiting: Faith and perseverance pay off.

ONLY BELIEVE, AND YOUR DREAM WILL COME TRUE.........

About the Author

Dr. Olean Hardaway Scott is an accomplished author of several short stories, producer, playwright, and songwriter. She writes and composes children's music. As a poet, she is listed in several anthologies. She has one book of poetry. Her mentor Gwendolyn Brooks was Poet Laureate of Illinois. She is a former teacher for the Chicago Board of Education. She has an honorary doctorate degree. She is an ordained minister of the Pentecostal Assemblies of the World, Inc. She resides in Chicago, Illinois.

Thanks for reading! If you loved the book and have a moment to spare, I would really appreciate a short review.

Made in the USA
Columbia, SC
07 November 2021